What is Adv

Advent is a season to prepare for Chris
thinking about the meaning of Jesus bir
Him coming again. The word advent means "to come. ᴛ...ᴜ ...
Book will help you think about Jesus' birth and His promises. Many
churches will celebrate each Sunday with special readings and
lighting a new candle each week on an Advent Wreath. Advent in
the church begins on the fourth Sunday before Christmas. The white
candle in the center symbolizing Christ, is circled by four other
candles, purple or pink.

The first candle means **HOPE** . For many years the faithful looked
forward to the coming of the Messiah.

The second candle means **LOVE.** We know that God is love.

The third candle means **JOY.** Prophecy has been fulfilled. The long-
awaited messiah has come.

The fourth candle means **PEACE.** Christ is the Prince of Peace.

The candles remind us of the light of God coming into the world, and
the light from the candles grows brighter as each week comes closer
to Christmas.

On December the first, you will begin your Advent Book. Each day you have a reading, sometimes a Bible verse, and an image to color. I pray that every Christmas will be special and that you will always remember the best gift we received was the gift of Jesus.

P.S. My father, Ed Nugent and I originally wrote this booklet over 20 years ago for my nieces and my parents' granddaughters. Our family had many Christmas traditions, though following Advent was not part of that tradition. As I grew older and became involved in churches that followed the Advent Season, I began to believe celebrating Advent with children, was an important tradition to have in the home. God Bless you and your family always.

Cheryl Ann

Scripture

ADVENT!

Exodus 29:45 I will live among the people of Israel and be their God.

Waiting For Christmas

Today is the first day of December. Christmas is coming! We know because our parents told us. But when will this happen? A long time ago, before Jesus was born, God told His people, we need a Savior and He promised He would send us this Savior. The people waited for that day. Today we start Advent, when we look forward to the day we celebrate Jesus birthday.

December 2

Scripture

II Samuel 22:17 He reached down from heaven and rescued me.

When we look at the stars in the sky, we cannot help but think WOW! For thousands of years people looked at the sky, prayed to God, and asked Him when would HE send the Saviour.

December 3

Scripture

Genesis 8: 10-11 Noah released the dove and the bird returned to him with a green olive leaf in his beak.

Long before Jesus came, the people of the earth were so evil, God said He would destroy everything. But there was one man who loved God and his name was Noah. God told him to build an ark, which is a big boat, and to take his family and two of every kind of animal inside the ark. God sent a flood, which destroyed everything, but He saved everyone and everything on the ark.

December 4

Scripture
Isaiah 53:6 All of us have strayed away like sheep. We have left God's path to follow our own way.

When God saved Noah, He told Noah to teach his children how to obey God. But they kept disobeying. God wanted everyone to obey His commandments, not to just please Him, but to make our lives much happier. God is the only one who can save us from our sin. He said we needed someone who would save and protect us. God protects us, like our earthly father should protect you. God is our Heavenly Father. Fathers are very important to God. There was a man named Joseph who was told by an angel, he was to be a father to a baby that was not his son but was God's son.

December 5

Scripture

Luke 1:37 For nothing is impossible with God.

Joseph had been asked to do a very important job. That job was to be the earthly father of God's Son. An angel told Mary she was going to have a baby. The angel said by a miracle God will be your child's father.

December 6

An angel came to Joseph to tell him Mary was going to have a baby. Now Joseph and Mary had decided to get married and have a family together, but they weren't married yet. This upset Joseph, but the angel said, "She will give birth to a Son, and He will be called "Emmanuel", which means God is with us. The angel told Joseph he was to take care of Mary and her son. So, Joseph and Mary were married and waited for the baby to be born.

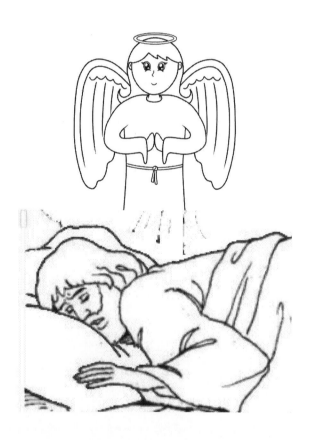

December 7

In a faraway land, there were wise men that studied the stars. One night they saw a new star, and they knew it meant a new king had been born. They wanted to see the king and they wanted to take gifts for the baby. They packed their gifts on the backs of the camels. The Bible names three gifts, so we know there were at least three wisemen, that went to see Jesus. They are sometimes called the magi. Most believe they came from the country that is now called Iran.

December 8

The first Wiseman carried gold on his camel. He said this is the perfect gift for a new king.

December 9

The second Wiseman packed frankincense. This was a very expensive gift, that was used when people worshiped God. They would burn this like a candle, and the fragrance would float up to God. Do you think this Wiseman knew he was taking a gift to God?

December 10

The third Wiseman packed a gift of myrrh. This was a very expensive perfume. But most people used this perfume after someone died. People would use perfumes to put on bodies before they were buried.

Don't you think this was a strange gift to take a baby? MAYBE SOMEHOW THIS WISEMAN KNEW WHEN THIS BABY GREW UP AND DIED HIS DEATH WOULD BE VERY IMPORTANT.

December 11

God says we are like sheep. Sheep are not very smart animals, and they must have a shepherd to guide and protect them. God said he would send a shepherd to His sheep.

December 12

Mary and Joseph lived in a town called Nazareth. God said the Saviour would be born in a town called Bethlehem. One day the Emperor said everyone had to go to the town where their parents had been born to be counted, and put on a list so the Emperor could know that you paid your taxes each year. Joseph's parents were from Bethlehem. Even though it was almost time for Mary to have her baby, Joseph had to follow the rule of the Emperor. Mary and Joseph started on their trip to Bethlehem.

December 13

The trip was hard because it was time for Mary to have her baby. But they had to follow the law. Joseph and Mary began their journey. Their donkey went clickity-clackety clickity-clackety down the road to Bethlehem. Today in a family car it would take about two hours to make the trip. For Mary and Joseph, it was probably seven to ten days.

December 14

When Mary and Joseph got to Bethlehem, there was no room left in the rooms to be rented. The only place they could stay was where the animals slept at night. In the stable, which is something like a barn, Joseph took some clean hay and made a soft bed for Mary to lay down. He used the manger, which was what the cow ate out of and put clean hay to make a bed for the baby . Mary was so tired, and it was time for her baby to be born.

December 15

God had made a promise to send His Son to earth, but it seemed very strange. Why was God going to have this special baby born in a barn?

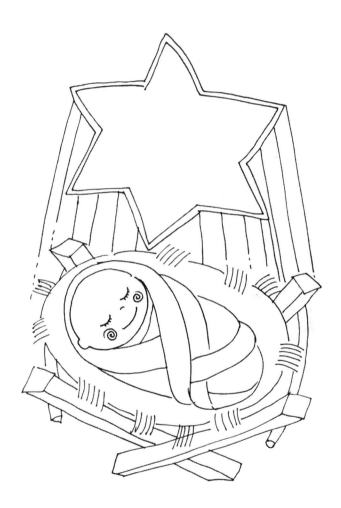

December 16

God always keeps His promise. He doesn't do things the way we usually think it should be done. But He knows what He is doing.

It was dark outside, but the shepherds out on the hills, were staying up to watch their sheep. Remember, sheep can get into a lot of trouble, if they are not watched. The angels in heaven were practicing for their first concert. God was telling them to get ready to sing. The audience were shepherds out on the hills.

December 17

I like to think about that night in the barn. Joseph had fed the donkey that brought them to Bethlehem and was feeding the other animals in the barn. I believe there was a dove sitting up near the top of the barn "cooing" and practicing to sing a special lullaby. Nearby stood the cow chewing his cud.

And then Mary brought forth her firstborn son and laid Him in the manger. Maybe Mary was remembering the day the angel told her she was going to have a special baby. Finally, the promise had come true. But this was a strange way for God to save the world. He sent a special baby to be born in a barn with the animals.

December 19

The wise men were on their trip following the star. We always say there were three wisemen, but the Bible does not say there were three, but we know there were three gifts.

December 20

We have been waiting for the promise. God said He would send a savior, but this sure isn't what I expected. What a surprise! I think everyone loves a surprise, even God.

December 21

We have heard about wisemen, angels, shepherds, animals, Joseph, Mary and a star. We decorate our houses with evergreens at Christmas to remind us even in the winter the evergreen stays green and beautiful. It is like God's promise, - no matter what happens, He will always keep his promise. Things might not happen like we thought, but God has the perfect plan and answer to all our lives and all our needs

December 22

Let's sing Silent Night

Silent Night, Holy Night
All is calm, all is bright
Round yon virgin, mother and child
Holy infant, so tender and mild
Sleep in heavenly peace.
Sleep in heavenly peace.

December 23

On the hills the shepherds did not know they were going to hear the first concert the angels ever sang. Suddenly, the sky filled with angels and they started to sing, "Glory to God in the highest, and on earth Peace, Good will toward Men."

December 24

And it came to pass, and she laid her firstborn son in the manger
and called his name Jesus. Tomorrow is Christmas. You will be so
busy with family and presents and eating. But don't forget, God
kept His promise because He loves you. Jesus is the most
important gift you will receive. Just like the gifts under the tree
you must open them so they can belong to you. So, don't just
think about Jesus, but accept the gift HE gave, by giving His son
to us and ask Jesus to live in your heart.

Let us pray.

Dear Jesus, thank you for sending Your Son to save me from my sins. Thank you for the gift and please live in my heart.

Sing Jesus Loves Me.

Jesus loves me, this I know,
for the Bible tells me so.
Little ones to him belong,
they are weak, but he is strong.
Yes, Jesus loves me
Yes, Jesus loves me
Yes, Jesus loves me.
The Bible tells me so.

Read the Christmas Story in **Luke Chapter 2** out of your Bible.

Note from the author:

Because we have been given the gift of God's love, we should then share this gift with all we encounter. My favorite yearly tradition is at my church on Christmas Eve. On Christmas Eve the service begins with the lighting of the four candles of the Advent Wreath, and then finally the tallest candle, the Christ Candle is lit. At the end of the service, the lights are dimmed and four elders (leaders) light their candle from the Christ Candle. The congregation begins singing Silent Night and each elder lights the candle of each person on the end of each row. Each participant then lights the candle of the person next to them, until all the candles are lit. As the elders lead us out of the church, into the darkness, onto the porch the congregation continues singing as they also exit the building. Finally, the musicians leave the building and the congregation continues to sing acapella (without instruments).

As we stand on the porch, with the stars overhead singing with our lit candles, a unique presence surrounds us. Many voices will cease, and instead silent tears will flow. Each year, I am moved again by the words of the song.

. . . . Glories stream from heaven afar, Heavenly hosts sing 'Alleluia! Christ the Savior is born . . . Silent night, holy night! Son of God, love's pure light, Radiant beams from Thy holy face with the dawn of redeeming grace. Jesus Lord, at Thy birth Jesus Lord, at Thy birth.

The night is dark, and our voices sing out to the people of our community. We send the message of hope, joy, peace and love. And our candles' flame came from the Christ Candle. This is a beautiful picture of Christmas. The city is in darkness, but it can be conquered with the light of Jesus.